龍
Dragon

兔
Rabbit

蛇
Snake

虎
Tiger

馬
Horse

牛
Ox

羊
Sheep

For nearly 5,000 years, the Chinese culture has organized time in cycles of twelve years. This Eastern calendar is based upon the movement of the moon (as compared to the Western calendar which follows the sun's path). The zodiac circle symbolizes how animals, which have unique qualities, represent each year. Therefore, if you are born in a particular year, then you share the personality of that animal. Now people worldwide celebrate this fifteen-day festival in the early spring and enjoy the start of another Chinese New Year.

鼠
Rat

猴
Monkey

豬
Pig

狗
Dog

雞
Rooster

☀ immedium

Immedium, Inc.
P.O. Box 31846
San Francisco, CA 94131
www.immedium.com

Text Copyright © 2012 Oliver Chin
Illustrations Copyright © 2012 Jennifer Wood

First hardcover edition published 2012.

Edited by Don Menn
Book design by Erica Loh Jones
Calligraphy by Lucy Chu

Printed in Singapore
10 9 8 7 6 5 4 3 2 1

Library of Congress Cataloging-in-Publication Data

Chin, Oliver Clyde, 1969-
  The year of the dragon : tales from the Chinese zodiac / by Oliver Chin ; illustrated by
Jennifer Wood. -- 1st hardcover ed.
       p. cm.
  Summary: Dominic the dragon befriends a boy named Bo as well as the other eleven
animals of the Chinese lunar calendar and helps them enter the annual village boat race.
Lists the birth years and characteristics of individuals born in the Chinese Year of the Dragon.
  ISBN 978-1-59702-028-2 (hardcover)
 [1. Dragons--Fiction. 2. Animals--Fiction. 3. Astrology, Chinese--Fiction.] I. Wood, Jennifer, ill.
II. Title.
  PZ7.C44235Ydo 2012
  [E]--dc23
                          2011015927

ISBN 10: 1-59702-028-1
ISBN 13: 978-159702-028-2

The Year of the Dragon

Tales from the Chinese Zodiac

Written by Oliver Chin
Illustrated by Jennifer Wood

immedium
Immedium, Inc.
San Francisco, CA

High amidst the mountain peaks, a pair of dragons lived. In their cave, they gently tended their first egg. Eventually its shell slowly began to crack. A whisper of smoke emerged and out peeked a baby!

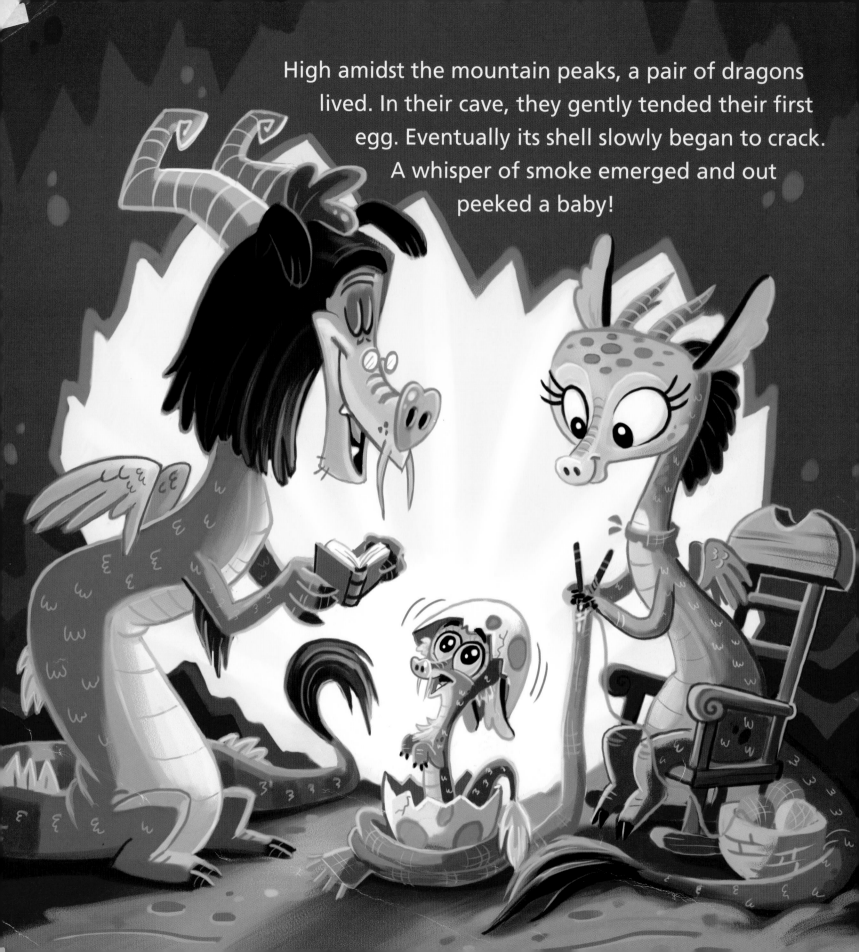

The proud parents scooped up their hatchling and named him "Dominic."

Papa Dragon beamed, "Now, Dom, you can roam the earth, sea, and sky." Perching outside, they showed him the world far below.

Gliding over hills and streams, the family spotted the Imperial Palace. The kind Emperor, Empress, and their court greeted them.

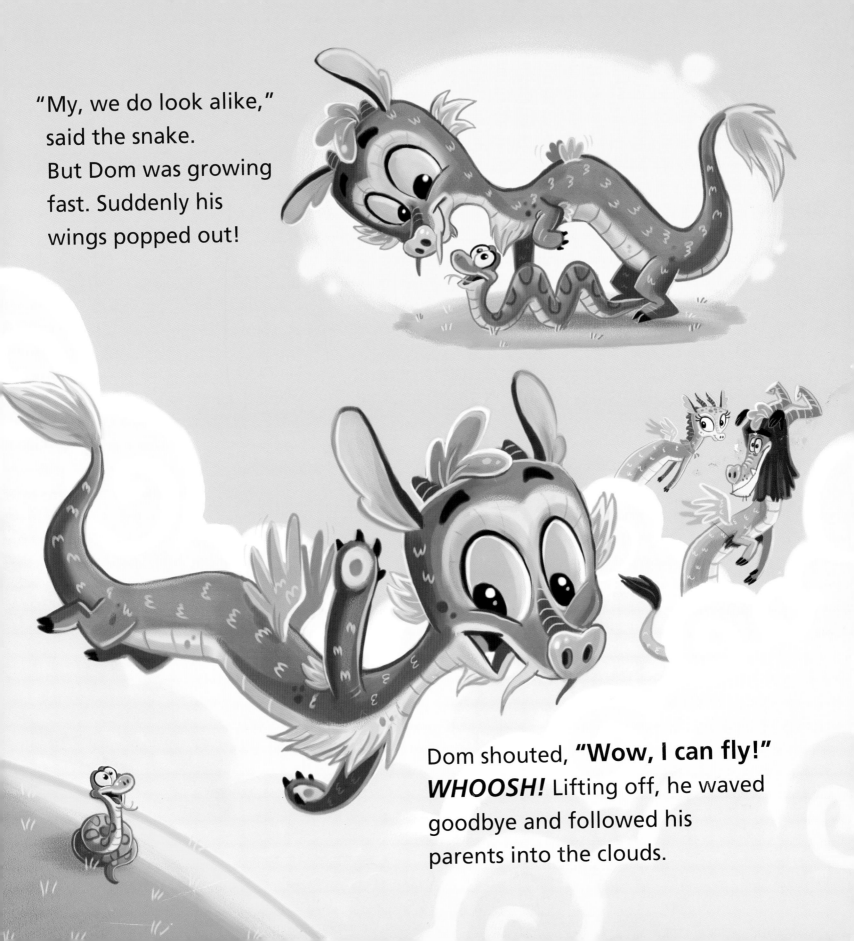

"My, we do look alike," said the snake. But Dom was growing fast. Suddenly his wings popped out!

Dom shouted, **"Wow, I can fly!"** *WHOOSH!* Lifting off, he waved goodbye and followed his parents into the clouds.

Mama reminded him,
"Remember, dragons are special.
No one can soar as swift
or swim as deep."

Papa puffed, "Who blows
the winds? Who commands
the rain? Who advises the
Emperor? We do!"

Indeed Dom learned that dragons could do things that others could not.

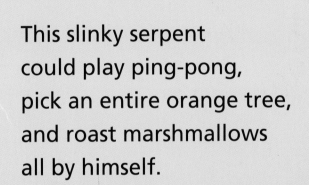

This slinky serpent could play ping-pong, pick an entire orange tree, and roast marshmallows all by himself.

One day, the boy named Bo invited Dom to a swimming party. The neighbors were excited to meet a dragon.

Yet everyone's attention soon turned to the noisy scene across the river.

Villagers beat drums and paddled long, narrow boats. Together they raced up and downstream. "That looks like fun," clucked the rooster.

"Hey, I see my uncle," said Bo. "Tomorrow, I'll ask him if we can join them."

The next day Dom met his new friends on the opposite shore. At the docks, Bo's uncle coached a group of people. The boy asked politely, "Good morning, Uncle! Can you teach us to paddle a boat, too?"

But the crowd laughed, and his uncle frowned. "Bo, we are busy practicing for the big race next week," he replied.

"We don't have time to teach you. So run along and play somewhere else."

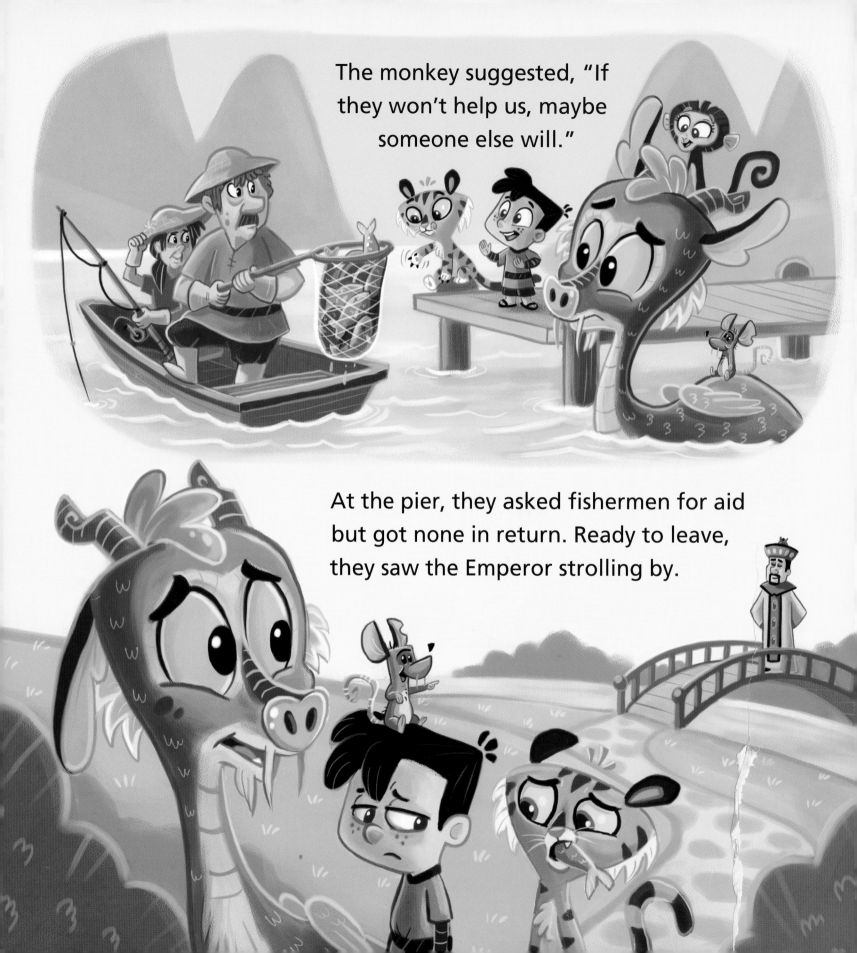

The monkey suggested, "If they won't help us, maybe someone else will."

At the pier, they asked fishermen for aid but got none in return. Ready to leave, they saw the Emperor strolling by.

The gang spurred Dom onward. **"Your highness, we want to paddle but have no boat,"** he explained. **"Could you help us?"**

"Dom," the Emperor replied, "as a favor to your parents, I'll lend you my spare canoe."

Overjoyed, they went to the palace, where a sleek ship awaited them on the royal lake. Happily they grabbed their gear. However, paddling was not as easy as they expected.

Either Dominic's paddle was too short or he was too long.

The last one in, the dragon could not fit his tail. Then the boat began to sway.

Everyone lost their balance and tipped over with a splash!

SPLASH!

The Emperor's team laughed as they floated by. "We are the champions and train all year," jeered the Royal Admiral. "Now you've sunk the Emperor's boat. Ha ha! Give up while you still can."

Bo and the animals were embarrassed.
The rat moaned,
"What should we do now?"

Not wanting to let them down,
Dom volunteered, **"I'll ask my
parents for advice. They are
wise and powerful."**

But Papa was not pleased.
"Dragons drive the winds
and waves," he fumed.
"We don't ride
on little boats."

Mama added,
"Dear, tell your friends
that you have better
things to do."

Soon Dom relayed the bad news,
"I guess I have to quit."

Bo sighed. "Maybe they're right. We're
too different after all." Dom shrugged
his shoulders and shrank sadly
into the shadows.

Gazing wistfully into the river, Dom noticed his reflection. The dragon was surprised that he shared many of his pals' qualities. Suddenly, he realized they had more in common than others thought.

He remembered what Mama and Papa had told him, "A dragon is the ruler of the water."

"Aha!" cried Dom. "I know what we can do!" Then he eagerly shared his plan.

The following morning, the villagers were startled to see the animals cruising by. "There are no rules against a *dragon boat*," sputtered Bo's uncle. "But Dom can't move his hands, feet, or wings!"

At practice, the rat steered, and Bo drummed the beat. The rest gradually matched their strokes.

Back and forth they pulled Dom. **WHOOSH!** After a long day, they were tired but eager for tomorrow's race.

The festival day had arrived!
Colorful banners decorated
the village and welcomed
teams from distant lands.

Visitors crowded the riverbanks and onlookers
marveled at this most unusual crew.

Among them were
two surprised guests.
Papa dragon roared,
"What does Dom
think he's doing?"

But Mama Dragon greeted Bo's
parents and whispered, "Wish the
boys good luck. They'll need it!"

The Empress banged the gong.
Bong! The big race had begun!

Paddles quickly beat the water.
The other teams sprinted ahead,
and the animals scrambled to
keep pace.

Reaching the halfway mark,
they trailed in last place.
"I have an idea," Dom shouted.
"Hold on tight!"

He took a deep breath,
sucked in his sides, and made
himself straighter than an arrow!

The "streamlined" dragon cut
through the water faster than before.
WHOOSH!

Like a fiery rocket, he sped down the
river. They passed Bo's uncle and
the other teams until only the
Imperial boat lay before them.

Suddenly Bo yelled,
"I see the Dragon Gate!"

They had almost caught up, but the finish was quickly approaching. They needed one last push, yet Dom was tiring from carrying them. What could he do?

Dom stretched his neck with a mighty roar. Both boats surged across the line. Who was first?

The judges huddled to determine the winner. Finally, the Emperor announced, "The dragon boat has won by a nose!"

The Emperor awarded a great
pearl to the unlikely champions.
"You were golden!" praised
Dom's parents.

The celebration
resounded toward
the heavens, and happy
dragons danced in delight.

Afterwards, Dom continued
to play with Bo and their pals. Wherever they went,
they learned how to be good sports and make
their parents proud of them in new ways.

From then on, Dom inspired many dragon boat races. And everyone from heaven below agreed that it was a magical year of the dragon.

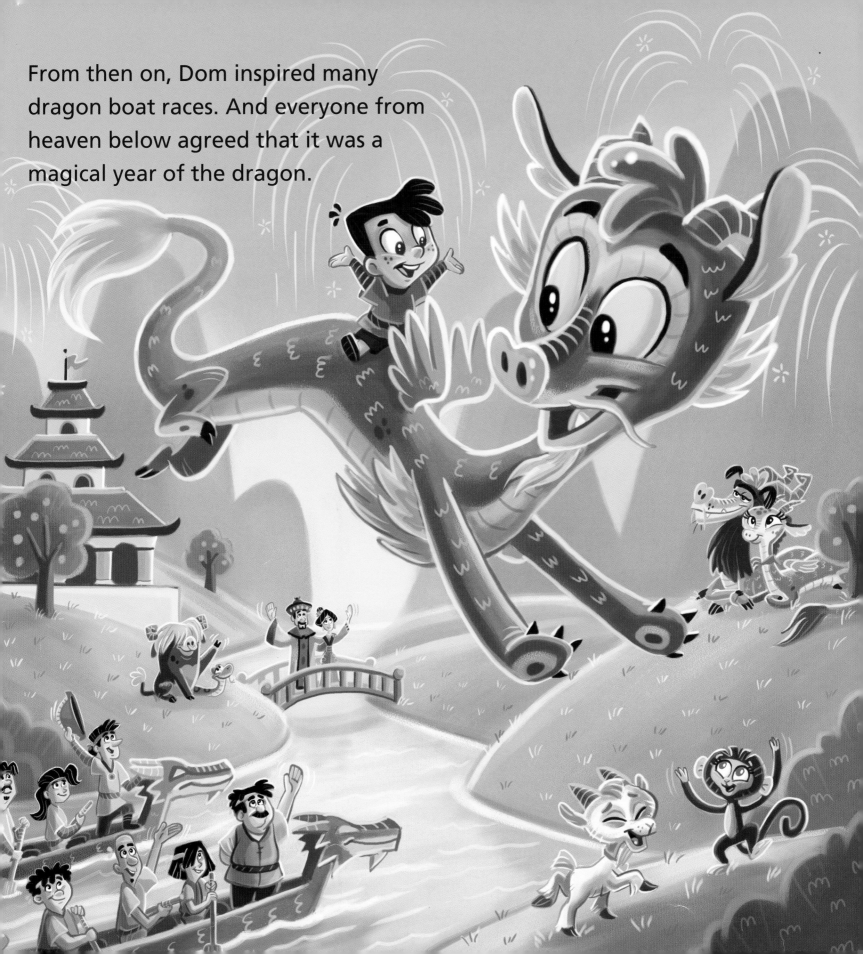

Dragon
1916, 1928, 1940, 1952, 1964, 1976, 1988, 2000, 2012, 2024

People born in the Year of the Dragon are strong and passionate, as well as idealistic and independent. But they can flare with emotion and be temperamental risk-takers. However, dragons are energetic and shoulder responsibility well, which make them the most reliable companions.